QUIZ BOOK

Derek O'Brien was born in Kolkata. He began his career as a journalist for *Sportsworld* magazine but soon shifted to advertising. After working for a number of very successful years as Creative Head of Oglivy, Derek decided to focus all his energy and talent in his passion–quizzing.

Today, Derek is Asia's best-known quizmaster and the CEO of Derek O'Brien & Associates. He is the host of the longest-running game show on Indian television, the Cadbury Bournvita Quiz Contest, for which he was voted the Best Anchor of a Game Show at the Indian Television Academy Awards for three years in a row. Always innovating, Derek is also credited with having conducted the first quiz on Twitter in 2010.

Derek has written over fifty bestselling reference, quiz and textbooks. In 2011, he was voted to the Rajya Sabha as a Member of Parliament (MP) and is the Leader of the Trinamool Congress Parliamentary Party in the Rajya Sabha.

Keep in touch with Derek on Twitter, where his handle is @quizderek.

QUIZ BOOK

DEREK O'BRIEN

RUPA

Published by
Rupa Publications India Pvt. Ltd 2017
7/16, Ansari Road, Daryaganj
New Delhi 110002

Sales Centres:
Allahabad Bengaluru Chennai
Hyderabad Jaipur Kathmandu
Kolkata Mumbai

ISBN: 978-81-291-4518-5

First impression 2017

10 9 8 7 6 5 4 3 2 1

The moral right of the author has been asserted.

SET A

TAKE YOUR PICK

1. In the Mahabharata, Duryodhana cried like which creature when he was born?
   a. Ass
   b. Horse
   c. Elephant

2. Which equation does David Bodanis call 'the world's most famous equation' in a biography of the equation?
   a. pr^2
   b. $E = mc^2$
   c. sxt

3. Which leader said 'Every blow aimed at me is a nail in the coffin of British imperialism'?
   a. Lal Bahadur Shastri
   b. Lala Lajpat Rai
   c. Bipin Chandra Pal

4. The roads of which Indian Union Territory were based on a unique plan called 7Vs by its original planner?
   a. Puducherry
   b. Andaman and Nicobar Islands
   c. Chandigarh

5. The name of which popular flavour comes from the Spanish word for 'pod'?
    a. Vanilla
    b. Strawberry
    c. Orange

6. What is the surname of Parvati in the *Harry Potter* series of books?
    a. Patil
    b. Peter
    c. Sarawati

7. Who is the author of *Natyashastra*?
    a. Bhasa
    b. Tulsidas
    c. Bharata Muni

8. Which Nobel Laureate's autobiography is *Freedom in Exile*?
    a. Nelson Mandela
    b. Dalai Lama
    c. Aung San Suu Kyi

9. What fraction of the Rajya Sabha retires every second year?
    a. Half
    b. One-third
    c. One-fourth

10. In a famous song from the film *Shree 420*, which accessory does Raj Kapoor describe as 'Roosi'?

a. Patloon
b. Topi
c. Joota

WHAT'S THE QUESTION

1. He was appointed editor of the newspaper, *Avanti!* in 1912.
2. They were a race of one-eyed giants; one of them was Polyphemus.
3. *Goal*
4. Bram Stoker
5. UN Day
6. The only country to have an actual building on its national flag.
7. Spirit of St Louis
8. It is a word puzzle with a grid of squares and blanks.
9. 10 Downing Street
10. Nephrons are the functional units of this organ.

MIXED BAG

1. Which is the largest country in Central America, with a coastline on both the Atlantic and the Pacific Ocean?
2. Who was the first Chairman of the Rajya Sabha?
3. Only one forest is the home of the Asiatic lion. Name it.
4. Which cricketer's autobiography is titled *Beyond 10,000, My Life Story*?
5. Which famous mausoleum was called 'a teardrop on

the cheek of time' by Rabindranath Tagore?

6. Who was issued India's first pilot's licence in 1929?

7. Who was the first National Professor of independent India?

8. Which was the first country to gain independence in the new millennium (2001–02)?

9. Who was awarded the Nobel Prize 'because of his profoundly sensitive, fresh and beautiful verse, by which, with consummate skill, he has made his poetic thought, expressed in his own English words, a part of the literature of the West'?

10. Which 1992 animated film had the tagline 'Imagine if you had three wishes, three hopes, three dreams and they all could come true'?

SPOT THE ANSWER

1. What is a plectrum used for?
   a. To strum a stringed instrument
   b. To break light into various colours
   c. To safeguard electrical appliances

2. Which cartoon character is called 'Skipper Skræk' in Denmark?
   a. Tintin
   b. Asterix
   c. Popeye

3. In medieval times, a knight threw down a gauntlet to challenge someone to a duel. Which part of his attire did a gauntlet refer to?

    a. The plume from his helmet
    b. His gloves
    c. His broadsword

4. Lexico was the original name for which board game?
    a. Snakes and ladders
    b. Scrabble
    c. Monopoly

5. The word 'solstice' comes from the Latin phrase meaning...
    a. A salt cellar
    b. A five-pointed star
    c. Sun stands still

CONFIDENCE ROUND

1. A chipmunk is a squirrel or a rabbit?
2. Which of these hill stations is located in Tamil Nadu: Ooty or Nainital?
3. What is the plural of Governor-General?
4. In 2001, which Australian became the youngest man to be ranked world number one in tennis?
5. The name of which Shah Rukh Khan starrer is shortened as *DDLJ*?
6. What kind of an animal was Black Beauty in the book of the same name?
7. Generally, how many wheels does a cycle rickshaw have?
8. What is Lord Krishna's panchajanya: conch shell or mace?

9. If a small circle has 360 degrees, how many degrees does a big circle have?
10. Which ruler died while leading his troops on the battlefield: Tipu Sultan or Humayun?

WHAT'S THE WORD

Set 1

1. Whose autobiography is called *The Fairy Tale of My Life*?
2. Which Pandava was also known as Dhananjaya?
3. Which is a flattened Indian bread: kalakand or naan?
4. Which cartoon character has nephews named Huey, Dewey and Louie?
5. Which Indian prime minister was born near Varanasi but died in the capital of Uzbekistan?
6. On a computer keyboard, what does 'Esc' stand for?
7. What's the word?

Set 2

1. Which book was written by Jayadeva: *Gita Govinda* or *Sur Sagar*?
2. *Olea europaea* is the scientific name of which tree?
3. In which country would you be if you spent takas?
4. Kargil is located in which Lok Sabha constituency?
5. Which channel is known as *La Manche* in French: English Channel or Dominica Channel?
6. Who is also known as the 'Tiger of Mysore'?
7. What's the word?

Set 3

1. Which month in the Gregorian calendar is named after Julius Caesar?
2. Who has served as the chief minister of Madhya Pradesh: Rabri Devi or Uma Bharti?
3. Triton is the largest satellite of which planet?
4. Panaji is the capital of which state of India?
5. The largest variety of which creature is the Komodo Dragon?
6. The Euro symbol is inspired by which Greek letter?
7. What's the word?

Set 4

1. Which state shares a border with Jharkhand: Bihar or Haryana?
2. Which actor is sometimes referred to as Khiladi Kumar?
3. Which famous South African leader is popularly known as Madiba?
4. In terms of average elevation, which is the highest continent in the world?
5. In war parlance, which three words do you use for the stretch of ground between two enemy lines?
6. Limba Ram represented India in which sport?
7. What's the word?

Set 5

1. What would a Scotsman do with a kilt: eat it or wear it?
2. Which Greek goddess shares her name with a part of the eye?
3. Which sport did Douglas Jardine play for England?

4. Which actress is married to Ajay Devgn?
5. What would you call the official residence of an ambassador?
6. Which card is used to predict one's future: tarot card or flash card?
7. What's the word?

MATHS AND IQ

1. OBMHNMHO : PANGOLIN :: SPQUNJRF : ?
2. Fill in the blanks with either addition, subtraction, multiplication or division to figure out the correct answer. Go sequentially from left to right without following BODMAS.

19		3		14		67	=	4

3. Nalini's total bill at a restaurant was ₹84, including the waiter's tip of 5 per cent. What was the bill amount excluding the waiter's tip?
4. Joy is taller than Rishi but shorter than Rinku. Rahul is taller than Manisha but shorter than Rishi. Who is the shortest of them all?
5. Fill in the blanks with either addition, subtraction, multiplication or division to figure out the correct answer. Go sequentially from left to right without following BODMAS.

38		14		21		5	=	9

VOCABULARY

1. Rearrange the letters of the word 'NONE' to get a

colourless gas.

2. Rearrange the letters of the word 'TIMER' to get a level of excellence.
3. Rearrange the letters of the word 'AGES' to get a religious person.
4. Read the word 'DRAW' backwards to get a room in a hospital.
5. Read the word 'AVID' backward to mean a female opera singer.

SPEED

1. Which rodent gives its name to a device attached to a computer?
2. Which war ended at 11 a.m. on the eleventh day of the eleventh month in 1918?
3. What milk-based product is the main ingredient of shrikhand?
4. What important part did James Phipps play in the history of medicine?
5. Which Pandava was also known as Dharmaputra?
6. Little Miss Muffet was afraid of spiders: serious or joking?
7. How many hands does an ambidextrous man have?
8. Is the Krishna river mainly in Andhra Pradesh or Tamil Nadu?
9. Who was Kareena Kapoor's grandfather?
10. With which art form is Anjolie Ela Menon associated?

ANSWERS

TAKE YOUR PICK

1. Ass
2. E=mc2
3. Lala Lajpat Rai
4. Chandigarh
5. Vanilla (The flavouring essence is derived from the pods of the vanilla orchid.)
6. Patil
7. Bharata Muni
8. Dalai Lama
9. One-third
10. Topi. The song was sung by Mukesh.

WHAT'S THE QUESTION

1. Who was Benito Mussolini?
2. Who were the Cyclopes? (singular: Cyclops)
3. Name Dhyan Chand's autobiography.
4. Who wrote *Dracula*?
5. What is 24 October celebrated as?
6. What is unique about the flag of Cambodia?
7. What was the name of Charles Lindbergh's aircraft in which he made the first solo transatlantic flight?
8. What is a crossword?
9. What is the address of the official office and residence of the prime minister of the United Kingdom?

10. What is kidney?

MIXED BAG

1. Nicaragua
2. Dr S. Radhakrishnan
3. Gir Forest in Gujarat
4. Allan Border
5. Taj Mahal
6. J.R.D. Tata
7. C. V. Raman
8. East Timor
9. Rabindranath Tagore
10. *Aladdin*

SPOT THE ANSWER

1. To strum a stringed instrument. It is a small bit of teardrop-shaped or triangular plastic.
2. Popeye
3. His gloves
4. Scrabble
5. Sun stands still

CONFIDENCE ROUND

1. Squirrel
2. Ooty
3. Governors-General
4. Lleyton Hewitt (Twenty years old)
5. *Dilwale Dulhania Le Jayenge*

6. Horse
7. Three
8. Conch shell
9. 360
10. Tipu Sultan

WHAT'S THE WORD

Set 1

1. Hans Christian Andersen
2. Arjuna
3. Naan
4. Donald Duck
5. Lal Bahadur Shastri
6. Escape
7. HANDLE

Set 2

1. *Gita Govinda*
2. Olive
3. Bangladesh
4. Ladakh
5. English Channel
6. Tipu Sultan
7. GOBLET

Set 3

1. July
2. Uma Bharti
3. Neptune
4. Goa

5. Lizard
6. Epsilon
7. JUNGLE

Set 4

1. Bihar
2. Akshay Kumar
3. Nelson Mandela
4. Antarctica
5. No man's land
6. Archery
7. BANANA

Set 5

1. Wear it
2. Iris
3. Cricket
4. Kajol
5. Embassy
6. Tarot card
7. WICKET

MATHS AND IQ

1. TORTOISE
2.

| 19 | Multiply | 3 | Plus | 14 | Minus | 67 | = | 4 |

3. ₹80
4. Manisha
5.

| 38 | Minus | 14 | Plus | 21 | Divide | 5 | = | 9 |

VOCABULARY

1. NEON
2. MERIT
3. SAGE
4. WARD
5. DIVA

SPEED

1. Mouse
2. World War I
3. Yoghurt/Curd
4. He was the boy who was given the first vaccination against smallpox by Edward Jenner.
5. Yudhisthir
6. Serious
7. Two
8. Andhra Pradesh
9. Raj Kapoor
10. Painting

SET B

TAKE YOUR PICK

1. According to Hindu mythology, who is the king of the yakshas?
    a. Kubera
    b. Skanda
    c. Yama

2. Which battle of Panipat was fought in the eighteenth century?
    a. First
    b. Second
    c. Third

3. What do Adelie penguins use to mark their nests?
    a. Pebbles
    b. Fish
    c. Feathers

4. The name of which food item comes from French words meaning 'baked twice'?
    a. Pizza
    b. Biscuit
    c. Cake

5. Which island of New York has four counties: Kings, Queens, Nassau and Suffolk?
   a. Long Island
   b. Loyalty Islands
   c. Falkland Islands

6. Which of these novels was written by Vikram Seth in verse?
   a. *The Glass Palace*
   b. *The God of Small Things*
   c. *The Golden Gate*

7. In the eighteenth century, which metal did King Louis XV of France declare as the only metal fit for a king?
   a. Platinum
   b. Silver
   c. Iron

8. Which Indian musician's father was the diwan of the Maharaja of Jhalawar?
   a. Pandit Ravi Shankar
   b. Ustad Zakir Hussain
   c. Pandit Shiv Kumar Sharma

9. If the colour of your school sweater is carmine, which colour is it?
   a. Deep red
   b. Deep blue
   c. Reddish-green

10. Which prime minister of India was around three years old when India became independent?
    a. V.P. Singh
    b. Rajiv Gandhi
    c. I.K. Gujral

WHAT'S THE QUESTION

1. It was Ian Fleming's only children's story.
2. Jacob Schick
3. It is a deadly disease caused by a bacteria, *Yersinia pestis*.
4. Kill Devil Hills
5. The Kauravas and Pandavas fought their great war here.
6. This fish is also known as 'caribe'.
7. His name is Kvack.
8. In 1862, he proposed the formation of voluntary relief societies in his book *A Memory of Solferino*.
9. He wrote *Indica*.
10. Emperor, Gentoo, Galapagos

MIXED BAG

1. On which African river is the Victoria Falls located?
2. Who was the only Indian Governor-General of independent India?
3. Which North American animal is referred to as the 'Silvertip Bear' because the tips of the hair on its body is silver-coloured?
4. Harsh Mankad represented India in the Davis Cup. In

which sport did his father, Ashok Mankad, represent India?

5. Which Indian city did Job Charnock 'find' in 1690?
6. What is a gentleman's agreement?
7. What does a car's radiator do?
8. Which famous book by Charles Dickens ends with the line: 'God bless us, everyone!'?
9. If you were visiting the archaeological areas of Pompeii, Herculaneum and Torre Annunziata, which country would you be in?
10. Who is the first actor to receive three consecutive Filmfare Awards in the Best Actor category?

SPOT THE ANSWER

1. The word simian is used to describe what?
   a. Sheep
   b. Snakes
   c. Monkeys

2. Hidrosis is the medical term for...
   a. Water in the brain
   b. Death due to drowning
   c. Perspiration

3. Which soccer star's reluctance to board a plane earned him the nickname 'The non-flying Dutchman'?
   a. Diego Maradona
   b. Eric Cantona
   c. Dennis Bergkamp

4. How is nyctalopia better known?
    a. Blindness
    b. Conjunctivitis
    c. Night blindness

5. What would the term 'Round Robin' best describe?
    a. A bird's nest
    b. A tournament in which each competitor plays in turn against every other
    c. A steamed pudding

CONFIDENCE ROUND

1. What would you call an ice cream that has fruits in it: candy or tutti-frutti?
2. Which is used to measure depth: a fathom or a farad?
3. What was held at Rajagriha, Vaishali, Pataliputra and Kundalavahana: Buddhist councils or appointment of Khalsa?
4. Which state is larger in area: Chhattisgarh or Madhya Pradesh?
5. How many sleeves do thirty white shirts have?
6. Which country's ancient emperors held the title Mikado?
7. In cricket, which continent has the most number of Test-playing nations?
8. What is the present name of the city where Aung San Suu Kyi was born?
9. A drake is a male horse: serious or joking?
10. What term is used to describe words or drawing scribbled on a wall: graffiti or cartoon?

WHAT'S THE WORD

Set 1

1. Which George was the first president of USA: Washington or Orwell?
2. *Electrophorus electricus* is the scientific name of which fish?
3. In Latin, what means forefinger: index or preface?
4. Alaknanda and Bhagirathi are the two main headstreams of which river?
5. Which part of Achilles' body was vulnerable (his weak point)?
6. Akhenaten was the father of which famous boy king?
7. What's the word?

Set 2

1. A high plateau named Lakshmi Planum is located on which planet?
2. The ancient Egyptians regarded the spherical bulb of which vegetable as a symbol of the universe?
3. In Yahoo.com, what does 'Y' in Yahoo stand for?
4. In *The Merchant of Venice*, from whom did Shylock wish to take his pound of flesh?
5. How do we know the rhizome of the plant *Zingiber officinale*?
9. Michael Vaughan captained which team in Test cricket?
7. What's the word?

Set 3

1. By what name is the Baha'i Temple in New Delhi

popularly known?

2. Which word is used to describe signatures given by celebrities to their fans?
3. The Sundarbans is situated in a valley or a delta?
4. What is the common name for a form of *seborrheic dermatitis* that affects the scalp?
5. What is the North American term for lift: elevator or subway?
6. If RAM stands for Random Access Memory, what does ROM stand for?
7. What's the word?

Set 4

1. Pushkar is famous for its camel fair. What is Etawah famous for?
2. Which Mughal emperor founded the city Allahabad?
3. Which country did Indira Gandhi call 'Chhota Bharat'?
4. If the letter 'T' in ET stands for terrestrial, what does the letter 'E' stand for?
5. Which event is celebrated in the first month of the Gregorian calendar: Republic Day or Independence Day?
6. According to legend, Newton discovered gravity after what fell on his head?
7. What's the word?

Set 5

1. A rabbit's tail is called a scut. What is a fox's tail called?
2. What is Udhagamandalam better known as: Ooty or Udaygiri?

3. Billie Jean King was professionally associated with which sport?
4. Which four-letter word is another name for 'making bread shorter': trim or trip?
5. Which part of the body does pneumonia mainly affect?
6. What does the 'e' in 'email' stand for?
7. What's the word?

MATHS AND IQ

1. From 2 to 49, if you add all the even multiples of 7, what will be your answer?
2. Fill in the blanks with either addition, subtraction, multiplication or division to figure out the correct answer. Go sequentially from left to right without following BODMAS.

18		2		11		95	=	4

3. Rearrange the letters of the words DAINTY and COIR to get the name of a book with meaningful words.
4. How many vowels appear immediately after a consonant in the word SUPERCALIFRAGILISTICEXPIALIDOCIOUS?
5. Fill in the blanks with either addition, subtraction, multiplication or division to figure out the correct answer. Go sequentially from left to right without following BODMAS.

14		4		6		10	=	6

VOCABULARY

1. Rearrange the letters of the word 'HART' to get the name of a desert.
2. Rearrange the letters of the word 'SLIP' to get a part of your face.
3. Rearrange the letters of the word 'GNU' to get a name of a weapon.
4. Read the word 'STAB' backward to get the plural of the name of a nocturnal mammal
5. Read the word 'DEER' backward to get a tall plant that grows in water

SPEED

1. Who was the last Mughal emperor of India?
2. Which prime minister of India wrote the book *The Insider*?
3. If your larynx was removed, you would suffer from which disability?
4. In 1980, the World Health Organization declared the world free of which disease?
5. What is the capital of the state of South Australia: Adelaide or Melbourne?
6. How many sides does a parallelogram have?
7. Sushmita Sen is Amartya Sen's daughter: serious or joking?
8. In 1982–83, which Indian batsman scored 1,182 runs in 11 away Test matches?
9. By what name is acetylsalicylic acid better known?
10. In nursery rhymes, what did Little Bo Peep lose?

ANSWERS

TAKE YOUR PICK

1. Kubera
2. Third. Ahmad Shah Abdali defeated the Marathas in 1761.
3. Pebbles
4. Biscuit
5. Long Island
6. *The Golden Gate*
7. Platinum
8. Pandit Ravi Shankar
9. Deep red
10. Rajiv Gandhi

WHAT'S THE QUESTION

1. What is *Chitty-Chitty-Bang-Bang*?
2. Who patented the first successfully manufactured electric razor?
3. What is plague?
4. Where did the Wright brothers' first successful flight take place?
5. What happened in Kurukshetra?
6. What is another name for Piranha?
7. In the comic strip *Hagar the Horrible*, what is the name of Hagar's family duck?

8. Who was Henri Dunant?
9. Who was Megasthenes?
10. Name three species of penguin.

MIXED BAG

1. Zambezi
2. C. Rajagopalachari
3. The grizzly bear
4. Cricket
5. Kolkata
6. An arrangement or understanding which is based upon the trust of both or all parties, rather than being legally binding.
7. It cools the engine.
8. *A Christmas Carol*
9. Italy
10. Dilip Kumar

SPOT THE ANSWER

1. Monkeys
2. Perspiration
3. Dennis Bergkamp. He played for the national football team of Netherlands, as well as for clubs like Ajax and Arsenal.
4. Night blindness
5. A tournament in which each competitor plays in turn against every other

CONFIDENCE ROUND

1. Tutti-frutti
2. Fathom
3. Buddhist Councils
4. Madhya Pradesh
5. Sixty
6. Japan
7. Asia
8. Yangon
9. Joking; it is a male duck
10. Graffiti

WHAT'S THE WORD

Set 1

1. Washington
2. Electric eel
3. Index
4. Ganges
5. His heel
6. Tutankhamen
7. WEIGHT

Set 2

1. Venus
2. Onion
3. Yet (YAHOO: Yet Another Hierarchical Officious Oracle)
4. Antonio
5. Ginger

9. England
7. VOYAGE

Set 3

1. Lotus Temple
2. Autograph
3. Delta
4. Dandruff
5. Elevator
6. Read Only Memory
7. LADDER

Set 4

1. Cattle fair
2. Akbar
3. Mauritius
4. Extra
5. Republic Day
6. An apple
7. CAMERA

Set 5

1. Brush
2. Ooty
3. Tennis
3. Trim
9. Lungs
6. Electronic
7. BOTTLE

MATHS AND IQ

1. 84
2.

18	Divided	2	Multiply	11	Minus	95	=	4

3. DICTIONARY
4. 13
5.

14	Minus	4	Multiply	6	Divided	10	=	6

VOCABULARY

1. THAR
2. LIPS
3. GUN
4. BATS
5. REED

SPEED

1. Bahadur Shah Zafar
2. P.V. Narasimha Rao
3. You would not be able to speak. The larynx is also called the 'voice box'.
4. Smallpox
5. Adelaide
6. Four
7. Joking
8. Mohinder Amarnath
9. Aspirin
10. Sheep

SET C

TAKE YOUR PICK

1. The name of which of these means 'man of the forest' in the Malay language?
   a. Orangutan
   b. Hedgehog
   c. Jaguar

2. Who was the British prime minister when India became independent?
   a. Clement Attlee
   b. Winston Churchill
   c. Harold McMillan

3. Which water body is called *Khalije Fars* in Persian and *Bahr Fars* in Arabic?
   a. Persian Gulf
   b. Gulf of Oman
   c. Red Sea

4. Which deity rides the elephant Airavat?
   a. Indra
   b. Vishnu
   c. Shiva

5. Which famous author wrote *Euclid and His Modern*

Rivals, a rare example of a humorous work concerning mathematics?
a. Charles Dickens
b. Mark Twain
c. Lewis Carroll

6. *Time*, one of M.F. Hussain's paintings, was inspired by the poem of which famous lyricist?
a. Gulzar
b. Javed Akhtar
c. Sameer

7. If a 'boomerang' is a throwing stick, what is a 'boomslang'?
a. An African snake
b. A bouncing ball
c. A firecracker

8. Which English cricketer as well as doctor was known for treating his poorer patients without charging a fee?
a. Sir Donald Bradman
b. Viv Richards
c. W.G. Grace

9. Which Bharat Ratna awardee produced the 1990 film *Lekin*?
a. Satyajit Ray
b. M.S. Subbalakshmi
c. Lata Mangeshkar

10. Which leader was also known as 'Frontier Gandhi'?
    a. Vallabhbhai Patel
    b. Khan Abdul Ghaffar Khan
    c. Bal Gangadhar Tilak

WHAT'S THE QUESTION

1. Clementines, navels and tangerines
2. It is the hardest tissue of the human body.
3. Barbara Millicent Roberts
4. He directed *Hazaar Chaurasi Ki Maa*.
5. This space term comes from the Latin words meaning 'space' and 'sailor'.
6. Filofax
7. It is a piece of metal or plastic used to help the foot into the shoe.
8. This portable stereo cassette player with headphones was invented in 1979.
9. It is called 'loo' in north India.
10. This unit of measurement comes from 'binary' and 'digit'.

MIXED BAG

1. Which river, called *Nahr Al-Urdun* in Arabic, shares its name with an Arab country of southwest Asia?
2. Which state in India has the largest number of seats in the Lok Sabha?
3. What is North America's largest rodent?
4. The first Indian chess Grandmaster was Vishwanathan Anand. Who is the second?

5. Who erected the Tower of Victory to commemorate his victory over Mahmud Khilji of Malwa in 1440?

6. By subtracting 32, dividing by 9 and multiplying by 5, what conversion can be made?

7. What is common to Cullinan, Star of the South and Great Mogul?

8. During World War II, who offered his people only 'blood, toil, tears and sweat' as they struggled to keep their freedom?

9. Which word would describe what limericks, haikus, sonnets and ballads are?

10. Which actress won her first National Award for Best Actress for the 1974 film *Ankur*?

SPOT THE ANSWER

1. The spacecraft Clementine discovered which of these, that increases the chances that humans may some day live on the moon?
   a. A golf ball
   b. A pond of frozen ice in a crater
   c. Traces of oxygen in the moon's atmosphere

2. Which of the seven ancient wonders of the world can still be seen today?
   a. Pyramids of Giza
   b. Hanging Gardens of Babylon
   c. Pharos of Alexandria

3. Who wrote *Man-Eaters of Kumaon*?
   a. Jim Corbett

b. Rohinton Mistry
c. Ruskin Bond

4. On what occasion did Sarojini Naidu write to Jawaharlal Nehru: 'Love to all and a kiss to the new soul of India'?
   a. When India achieved independence
   b. On the birth of Indira Gandhi
   c. At the start of the Quit India Movement

5. In *Gulliver's Travels*, what caused the war between Lilliput and Blefuscu?
   a. Whether to break the broad or narrow end of an egg
   b. The gold in Gulliver's ship
   c. A land dispute

CONFIDENCE ROUND

1. Which dynasty was founded by Hasan Gangu in 1347?
2. In the film *The Lion King*, Simba was a lion. What kind of a creature was Timon?
3. Lungfish really have lungs: serious or joking?
4. Which country did gymnast Nadia Comaneci represent at the Olympics: USA or Romania?
5. Which Shakespearean play is also known as *The Scottish Play*?
6. If Christmas is associated with cakes, what food item is Good Friday associated with?
7. What does a chauffeur do for a living?

8. Which hill station is in Uttarakhand: Mussoorie or Manali?
9. In India, how are 'cabs' mostly known?
10. Callisto and Europa are moons of Jupiter: serious or joking?

WHAT'S THE WORD

Set 1

1. Which is an Arab ship with a large triangular sail: dhow or kayak?
2. What is the colour of the disc on the National Flag of Bangladesh?
3. The Romans called which fruit *malum praecocum* or 'the apple that ripens early'?
4. Which animal was earlier called 'camelopard': giraffe or leopard?
5. If Wilbur was one of the famous Wright Brothers, who was the other?
6. In which city are the headquarters of the United Nations located?
7. What's the word?

Set 2

1. Rubric or a heading on a document was originally written in which ink: Red or Blue?
2. Which mythical animal is typically represented as a horse with a single straight horn projecting from its forehead?
3. Which insects are kept in an apiary?

4. What colour cap is awarded to English Test cricketers: blue or yellow?
5. When you inhale, does your chest expand or contract?
6. Which is the largest country in the world in terms of area?
7. What's the word?

Set 3

1. Give another name for a Mexican lion or cougar beginning with the letter 'P'.
2. Complete this trio of Indian music composers: Shankar, _____ and Loy.
3. Big Ears and Mr Plod the policeman are friends of which fictional character?
4. Who is the first Indian to claim a hat-trick in an ODI match?
5. 'Thou art the ruler of the minds' (when translated) is the opening line of the National Anthem of which country?
6. Does Brahma sit on a lotus or a rose?
7. What's the word?

Set 4

1. Which festival connects Bohag or Rongali, Kati or Kangali, and Magh or Bhogali?
2. A German submarine used in the First or Second World War was called a U-boat or a Merchant ship?
3. *Back to the Mark* is the autobiography of which former fast bowler?
4. Which Hindu god is called Vighna Harta as he removes obstacles?

5. An extremely expensive possession to keep is often referred to as 'a white _____'.
6. Name the second largest US state in terms of area. (Hint: Austin is the capital and Houston is its largest city.)
7. What's the word?

Set 5

1. Which fibre grows on the seed of a variety of plants of the genus *Gossypium*?
2. What is the first letter of the Greek alphabet called?
3. In which present-day state is the historical site of Haldighati located?
4. Which Indian gallantry award literally means 'Wheel of the Ultimate Brave'?
5. More than 600 places in Australia are named after which flightless bird?
6. Was the film *Roja* first made in Hindi or Tamil?
7. What's the word?

MATHS AND IQ

1. How is Tanu's paternal grandfather's only sister's only brother's son related to Tanu?
2. Fill in the blanks with either addition, subtraction, multiplication or division to figure out the correct answer. Go sequentially from left to right without following BODMAS.

7		3		5		41	=	9

3. A man ate 100 mangoes in 5 days. Each day, if he ate 6 more than the previous day, how many did he eat

the first day?

4. Fill in the blanks with either addition, subtraction, multiplication or division to figure out the correct answer. Go sequentially from left to right without following BODMAS.

26		23		3		5	=	14

5. In a code language, 'poka beri' means 'fine cloth', 'meta sira' means 'clear water' and 'lona sira beri' means 'fine clear weather'. Which word in that language means 'weather'?

VOCABULARY

1. Rearrange the letters of the word 'DONE' to get a part of a plant.
2. Rearrange the letters of the word 'LURE' to get a word that means king's reign.
3. Rearrange the letters of the word 'ERASE' to get an Indian garment.
4. Rearrange the letters of the word LIAR to get the name of a place where wild animals live.
5. Read the word DRAW backward to mean sections in a hospital.

SPEED

1. Tanuja is Kajol's sister, mother or aunt?
2. Who was introduced as Mickey Mouse's pet blood-hound in *The Chain Gang*?
3. The India Gate is in Mumbai: agree or disagree?

4. Is Pongal an important festival of Bihar or Tamil Nadu?
5. How many collars do thirty wet shirts have?
6. Who is the heroine of *Much Ado About Nothing*: Viola or Beatrice?
7. If the 1996 cricket World Cup was called the Wills World Cup, what were the World Cups of 1975, 1979 and 1983 called?
8. How long is a Guinea pig's tail?
9. Which reed did the ancient Egyptians make into a type of paper?
10. In cricket, a score of 0 is called a duck or a chicken?

ANSWERS

TAKE YOUR PICK

1. Orangutan
2. Clement Attlee
3. Persian Gulf
4. Indra
5. Lewis Carroll
6. Javed Akhtar
7. An African snake
8. W.G. Grace
9. Lata Mangeshkar
10. Khan Abdul Ghaffar Khan

WHAT'S THE QUESTION

1. Name different varieties of oranges.
2. What is enamel?
3. What is Barbie's full name?
4. Who is Govind Nihalani?
5. What is the meaning of the word 'astronaut'?
6. What is the name given to a portable loose-leaf notebook?
7. What is a shoe horn?
8. When was the walkman invented?
9. In summer, which hot, dry north Indian wind scorches the crops and grass?
10. What is a 'bit'?

MIXED BAG

1. Jordan
2. Uttar Pradesh
3. Beaver
4. Dibyendu Barua
5. Maharana Kumbha
6. Fahrenheit to Celsius
7. They are all diamonds.
8. Sir Winston Churchill
9. Poems
10. Shabana Azmi

SPOT THE ANSWER

1. A pond of frozen ice in a crater
2. Pyramids of Giza
3. Jim Corbett
4. On the birth of Indira Gandhi
5. Whether to break the broad or narrow end of an egg

CONFIDENCE ROUND

1. The Bahmani kingdom
2. Meerkat
3. Serious
4. Romania
5. *Macbeth*
6. Hot cross buns
7. Drive a car
8. Mussoorie

9. Taxis
10. Serious

WHAT'S THE WORD

Set 1

1. Dhow
2. Red
3. Apricot
4. Giraffe
5. Orville
6. New York City
7. DRAGON

Set 2

1. Red
2. Unicorn
3. Bees
4. Blue
6. Expand
6. Russia
7. RUBBER

Set 3

1. Puma
2. Ehsaan
3. Noddy
4. Chetan Sharma
5. India
6. Lotus
7. PENCIL

Set 4

1. Bihu
2. U-boat
3. Dennis Lillee
4. Ganesha
5. Elephant
6. Texas
7. BUDGET

Set 5

1. Cotton
2. Alpha
3. Rajasthan
4. Param Vir Chakra
5. Emu
6. Tamil
7. CARPET

MATHS AND IQ

1. Father

2.

7	Plus	3	Multiply	5	Minus	41	=	9

3. 2

4.

26	Minus	23	Multiply	3	Plus	5	=	14

5. Iona

VOCABULARY

1. NODE
2. RULE

3. SAREE
4. LAIR
5. WARD

SPEED

1. Mother
2. Pluto
3. Disagree. It is in New Delhi
4. Tamil Nadu
5. Thirty
6. Beatrice
7. Prudential Cup
8. It does not have a tail. It is not visible externally.
9. Papyrus
10. Duck

SET D

TAKE YOUR PICK

1. Which is the only member of the cat family that hunts primarily during the day?
   a. Cheetah
   b. Lion
   c. Tiger

2. Which Portuguese explorer became a page to Queen Leonor, wife of John II, in Lisbon at an early age?
   a. Ferdinand Magellan
   b. Christopher Columbus
   c. Marco Polo

3. According to Hindu mythology, which was the second of the four yugas?
   a. Kali yuga
   b. Treta yuga
   c. Dvapara yuga

4. By what Indian name is 'sweet golden yoghurt' better known?
   a. Shrikhand
   b. Kheer
   c. Paneer

5. Which planet's most conspicuous feature is the Caloris Basin?
   a. Mars
   b. Jupiter
   c. Mercury

6. Which musical instrument did Guru Nanak's friend and companion Mardana play?
   a. Sitar
   b. Tanpura
   c. Rabab

7. Lake Kawaguchi is noted for reflecting the image of which mountain in its waters?
   a. Mount Fuji
   b. Mount Kilimanjaro
   c. Mount Etna

8. In which of these sports is the term 'fluke' most likely to be used?
   a. Billiards
   b. Football
   c. Hockey

9. Which gemstone is commonly judged by the 'four Cs': carat, clarity, colour and cut?
   a. Opal
   b. Diamond
   c. Amethyst

10. Which film starring Aishwarya Rai is based on O. Henry's short story, *The Gift of the Magi*?
    a. *Khaki*
    b. *Bride and Prejudice*
    c. *Raincoat*

WHAT'S THE QUESTION

1. Alexander Selkirk, a Scottish sailor, provided the inspiration for the story.
2. The group of twelve who decide if a person is guilty or innocent.
3. In the Mahabharata, she was Abhimanyu's mother.
4. It is the only country to have a non-rectangular or square flag.
5. The fattest of Robin Hood's merry men.
6. A game in which players buy and sell houses and hotels.
7. Mount Pidurutalagala is the highest point of this country.
8. This horizontal bone connects the shoulder blade and the sternum.
9. This machine's name comes from Latin, meaning 'to make similar'.
10. This Mughal emperor, the son of Shah Jahan, called himself Alamgir (world conqueror).

MIXED BAG

1. It lies in Australia and rises 335 metres abruptly from the sand dune plains, about 450 km from Alice

Springs. It is perhaps the world's largest monolith. What is it?

2. Who was the first Communist chief minister in India?

3. In 2001, whose record did Mohammed Ashraful of Bangladesh break, to become the youngest cricketer to score a Test century?

4. Which city would you be in if you passed under the famous Bridge of Sighs?

5. Who has published a book of poems and reflections titled *Dancing the Dream*?

6. Which historical place connects Ibrahim Lodi's battle against Babur in 1526, Akbar's victory over Hemu in 1556 and Ahmad Shah Abdali's conflict with the Marathas in 1761?

7. In 1864, who became a resident master in Elgin's Weston House Academy in Scotland?

8. Who is common to Dasher, Dancer, Prancer, Vixen, Comet, Cupid, Donner/Donder, Blitzen and Rudolph?

9. The Swiss Guards are responsible for the safety of which religious head?

10. 'Four legs good, two legs bad' is the essence of animalism as described in which book?

SPOT THE ANSWER

1. The Tibetans call it Chomolungma, meaning 'Goddess Mother of the World'. What is its English name?
   a. Yak
   b. Mount Everest
   c. Godwin-Austen or K2

2. Her native name was Ma Tint Tint. She later became Usha. Who was she?
   a. P.T. Usha
   b. India's former first lady Usha Narayanan
   c. Usha Mangeshkar

3. Where might you see Nishi warriors with hornbill caps and knives in monkey-skin scabbards?
   a. Russia
   b. Madhya Pradesh
   c. Arunachal Pradesh

4. In 1524, which famous explorer was buried in St Francis Church, Fort Kochi?
   a. Ferdinand Magellan
   b. Christopher Columbus
   c. Vasco da Gama

5. Traditionally, who uses a gold broom and acts as 'sweeper to the gods' at the Puri Rath Yatra?
   a. The head priest
   b. Gajapati Maharaja of Puri
   c. The chief minister of Odisha

CONFIDENCE ROUND

1. In tennis, which is the first Grand Slam tournament played in a calendar year: US Open or Australian Open?
2. Which is usually found underwater: a sloth or an oyster?

3. In Literature, the expression 'open sesame', is associated with: Aladdin or Ali Baba?
4. Who was the famous mother of Irene Joliot?
5. Who starred in the film *Khakee*: Amitabh Bachchan or Aamir Khan?
6. Which is the twin city of Hyderabad: Aurangabad or Secunderabad?
7. Which dance form originated in Kerala: Theyyam or Chhau?
8. Apart from 'Entry' which other signage starting with 'E' are you most likely to see inside a cinema?
9. Which Japanese military attack on 7 December 1941 was code-named Operation Z?
10. What number shirt did Pele wear during his football career?

WHAT'S THE WORD

Set 1

1. Give a three-letter word for a large, strong African antelope that has the Afrikaans name 'wildebeest'?
2. Pokhran is in which Indian state?
3. Which colour comes between yellow and red in a rainbow?
4. Which five letter word relates to a town or a city: urban or rural?
5. The Arctic Circle is near the North Pole or the South Pole?
6. Which cartoon duck celebrated his 80th birthday in 2014?
7. What's the word?

Set 2

1. Which is a closer relative of the giraffe: okapi or zebra?
2. The playing time of the full version of the Indian National Anthem is approximately how many seconds?
3. In the language panel of a contemporary banknote, in how many languages is its denomination written?
4. The name of which fabric literally means 'fasten, tie' in Malay: Ikat or Pashmina?
5. In America, the standard grid size of what is 15 by 15 squares for daily newspapers and 21 by 21 squares for Sunday editions?
6. Tiny bones called ossicles are part of which organ of your body?
7. What's the word?

Set 3

1. Who is the author of the book *The Athenian Constitution*: Socrates or Aristotle?
2. What is the highest number on a telephone keypad?
3. According to Lokmanya Tilak's famous slogan, what was his birthright?
4. In which state is Jaldapara Wildlife Sanctuary located?
5. The injury which is common in people who play a lot of tennis or other racquet sports is called tennis _____.
6. Which singer is famous for his song 'Bulla Ki Jana Main Kaun'?
7. What's the word?

Set 4

1. Which item of cutlery with prongs is also something you might come across on the road?
2. Shweta Nanda is the sister of which famous bollywood actor?
3. Which of these is a form of pasta: macaroni or semolina?
4. Which of these has Sachin Tendulkar played more of: Tests or One Day Internationals?
5. What is the capital of Mongolia?
6. What instrument does Ustad Hafiz Ali Khan's famous son play?
7. What's the word?

Set 5

1. Which famous Italian food item literally means 'pie': pasta or pizza?
2. Which animal has the largest brain of any land mammal: tiger or elephant?
3. Who has written the national anthem of Bangladesh?
4. Gandhinagar lies on the right bank of which river?
5. If *The Pickwick Papers* was Charles Dickens' first novel, which was his second?
6. In Hindu mythology, what is the name of Shiva's bull?
7. What's the word?

MATHS AND IQ

1. RAINBOW : WBIRANO : : ? : DAOLEPR
2. Fill in the blanks with either addition, subtraction, multiplication or division to figure out the correct

answer. Go sequentially from left to right without following BODMAS.

12		4		15		7	=	9

3. Fardeen likes to eat apples and oranges. Rintu likes to eat bananas and oranges, Anushua likes only oranges. Pritam eats only apples. Which fruit is liked by only one person?

4. Fill in the blanks with either addition, subtraction, multiplication or division to figure out the correct answer. Go sequentially from left to right without following BODMAS.

16		5		69		3	=	14

5. The first page of a book is on the right hand side and pages numbered 22 to 30 are missing. How many leaves have been torn out?

VOCABULARY

1. Rearrange the letters of the word 'SALE' to get the name of a famous lioness.

2. Rearrange the letters of the word 'LUMP' to get a fruit.

3. Rearrange the letters of the word 'MORE' to get a city.

4. Read the word 'FLOG' backward to get the name of a game.

5. Read the word 'LAP' backward to mean a friend.

SPEED

1. Which liquid do we generally have with cornflakes?
2. In 1901, who started a school at Shantiniketan named Bramhachari Ashram?
3. If Agatha Christie created Miss Marple, who created Hercule Poirot?
4. The Swiss flag consists of which two colours?
5. Who composed the music for the 1995 film *Rangeela*?
6. What is the STD code for Mumbai?
7. Where do women wear mascara?
8. *The Fellowship of the Ring* was initially published as the first part of which novel?
9. In which city is the Eden Gardens located?
10. The spacecraft Luna 2 landed on which celestial body?

ANSWERS

TAKE YOUR PICK

1. Cheetah
2. Ferdinand Magellan
3. Treta yuga
4. Shrikhand; indigenous to Maharashtra and Gujarat
5. Mercury
6. Rabab
7. Mount Fuji
8. Billiards
9. Diamond
10. *Raincoat*

WHAT'S THE QUESTION

1. Who inspired Daniel Defoe to write *Robinson Crusoe*?
2. What is a jury?
3. Who was Subhadra?
4. What is special about the flag of Nepal?
5. Who was Friar Tuck?
6. What is Monopoly?
7. What is Sri Lanka's highest point called?
8. What is the clavicle in the human body?
9. How did the fax machine get its name?
10. Who was Aurangzeb?

MIXED BAG

1. Ayers Rock
2. E.M.S. Namboodiripad
3. Mushtaq Mohammad, 17 years and 78 days
4. Venice
5. Michael Jackson
6. Panipat
7. Alexander Graham Bell
8. Santa Claus
9. The Pope
10. *Animal Farm* by George Orwell

SPOT THE ANSWER

1. Mount Everest
2. India's former first lady Usha Narayanan
3. Arunachal Pradesh
4. Vasco da Gama
5. Gajapati Maharaja of Puri

CONFIDENCE ROUND

1. Australian Open; it is usually played in the month of January.
2. An oyster
3. Ali Baba
4. Marie Curie
5. Amitabh Bachchan
6. Secunderabad
7. Theyyam

8. Exit
9. Pearl Harbour
10. Ten

WHAT'S THE WORD

Set 1

1. Gnu
2. Rajasthan
3. Orange
4. Urban
5. North Pole
6. Donald Duck
7. GROUND

Set 2

1. Okapi
2. Fifty-two
3. Fifteen
4. Ikat
5. Crossword
6. Ear
7. OFFICE

Set 3

1. Aristotle
2. Nine
3. Swaraj
4. West Bengal
5. Elbow
6. Rabbi Shergill

7. ANSWER

Set 4

1. Fork
2. Abhishek Bachchan
3. Macaroni
4. One Day Internationals
5. Ulaanbaatar
6. Sarod (Ustad Amjad Ali Khan)
7. FAMOUS

Set 5

1. Pizza
2. Elephant
3. Rabindranath Tagore
4. Sabarmati
5. *Oliver Twist*
6. Nandi
7. PERSON

MATHS AND IQ

1. LEOPARD
2.

12	Multiply	4	Plus	15	Divide	7	=	9

3. Banana
4.

16	Multiply	5	Minus	69	Plus	3	=	14

5. 5

VOCABULARY

1. ELSA

2. PLUM
3. ROME
4. GOLF
5. PAL

SPEED

1. Milk
2. Rabindranath Tagore
3. Agatha Christie
4. White and red
5. A.R. Rahman
6. 022
7. Eyes
8. *Lord of the Rings*
9. Kolkata
10. Moon

SET E

TAKE YOUR PICK

1. The name of which breed of dog comes from a German word meaning 'splash in water'?
   a. Boxer
   b. Poodle
   c. Doberman

2. In Hindu mythology, who received the title of Indrajit after he defeated Indra in a battle?
   a. Vibhishana
   b. Meghnad
   c. Kumbhakarna

3. During his last days, who became the guardian of the ruler of Travancore?
   a. Raja Ravi Varma
   b. M.F. Hussain
   c. Jamini Roy

4. In 1982, the advent of colour television coincided with which event in India?
   a. First General Elections
   b. First Census
   c. Asian Games inauguration

5. In 1933, what name did Rabindranath Tagore choose for the baby of his secretary's daughter?
   a. Amartya
   b. Satyajit
   c. Kishore

6. What is the national tree of Pakistan?
   a. Deodar
   b. Peepal
   c. Cypress

7. Penne, bow and fusilli are different kinds of which tasty food item?
   a. Ice cream
   b. Cheese
   c. Pasta

8. What is the term used to describe an entertainer who makes a wooden dummy appear to speak?
   a. Puppeteer
   b. Veterinarian
   c. Ventriloquist

9. Which natural process gets its name from the Greek words meaning 'light' and 'together'?
   a. Evaporation
   b. Photosynthesis
   c. Respiration

10. *Krrish* is the sequel to which Bollywood blockbuster?
    a. *Koi Mil Gaya*

b. *Kabhi Khushi Kabhie Gham*
c. *Mission Kashmir*

WHAT'S THE QUESTION

1. This part of a radio is also called an aerial.
2. A mollusc with three hearts and eight arms.
3. Elephants use this for smelling, breathing, trumpeting, drinking and also to grab things.
4. In chess notation, this piece is designated as N.
5. Approximately, 78 per cent nitrogen, 21 per cent oxygen and 1 per cent other gases
6. The letters Q, U, X, Y and Z are never used in its naming by the World Meteorological Organization.
7. In the Ramayana, he was Bharata and Lakshmana's father.
8. Zambia gets its name from this waterbody.
9. The famous Calico Museum is located in this city.
10. This actor's original name was Shivaji Rao Gaekwad.

MIXED BAG

1. 'Checkpoint Charlie' was a checkpoint on the border of which two European cities? (Hint: The checkpoint no longer exists.)
2. What are you most likely to find inside a 'mermaid's purse'?
3. Who was the first recipient of the Rajiv Gandhi Khel Ratna Award?
4. In Einstein's equation $E=mc^2$, what does 'c' stand for?
5. The flag of which country depicts a crossed rifle and

    hoe in black superimposed on an open white book?

6. Which US president adopted 'White House' as the official name of the Executive Mansion?

7. What was W.B. Yeats referring to when he said: 'I have carried the manuscripts of these translations around with me for days, reading it in trains or on the top of buses and in restaurants. I have often had to close it lest some stranger should see how much it moved me.'

8. Who was the first Indian woman to become the president of the Indian National Congress?

9. The Bimal Roy-directed film *Do Bigha Zamin* got its name from a poem by which famous author?

10. What was constructed by Emperor Akbar on the remains of an ancient site known as Badalgarh?

SPOT THE ANSWER

1. What is the difference between kajal and kohl?
    a. Kajal is for the eyelashes while kohl is for the eyebrows
    b. Kajal is for adults, kohl is for children
    c. There is no difference

2. According to Aristotle, what is the best provision for old age?
    a. Money
    b. Education
    c. Children

3. Which phrase is used to describe a prime minister's

inner cabinet or most trusted members?
a. Bedroom cabinet
b. Shower cabinet
c. Kitchen cabinet

4. Which children's novel by Dodie Smith is also a Walt Disney film?
a. *The Little Mermaid*
b. *The Lion King*
c. *101 Dalmatians*

5. How is Kongzi better known to us?
a. Confucius
b. Dalai Lama
c. Bruce Lee

CONFIDENCE ROUND

1. In which Shakespearean play would you meet Ariel, Prospero, Miranda and Caliban?
2. Which flavouring agent is called *banira* in Japanese?
3. Which is the first city to have hosted the Winter Olympic Games twice?
4. The Niagara Falls partly lies in: Canada or Mexico?
5. The deficiency of which element is the cause of the most common type of goitre?
6. Who wrote a treatise on geometry titled *Elements*: Euclid or Aristotle?
7. In which state is the Keoladeo National Park located?
8. Raj Ghat is the samadhi of which leader?
9. Which Indian philosopher started an ashram in

Puducherry: Sri Aurobindo or Ramanuja?
10. The Bara Imambara is in which Indian city: Panjim or Lucknow?

WHAT'S THE WORD

Set 1

1. Who composed the music for the film *Roja*?
2. In China, *mian pian* is a kind of noodle or boat?
3. With which classical danceform would you associate the name of Birju Maharaj?
4. Lao is the official language of which Asian country?
5. Which reddish-gray-coloured worm is often called a nightcrawler in the United States?
6. Mats Wilander was a world-class player in which sport?
7. What's the word?

Set 2

1. In the Ramayana, which demon was the eldest son of Vishravas and Kaikasi?
2. The brown bear and the Himalayan bear are both found in India. In which country would you find a koala bear in the wild?
3. Who played the title role in the 1959 film *Ben-Hur*?
4. Which danceform orginated in North India: Kathak or Kuchpudi?
5. In Indian football if the 'Red and Gold' is up against the 'Maroon and Green', then which two teams are playing?
6. In which Indian state is the Meenakshi Temple located?

7. What's the word?

Set 3

1. Are your vocal chords in your larynx or your trachea?
2. What is a wooden frame for holding an artist's work while it is being painted or drawn called?
3. In Norse mythology, Mjölnir is the hammer of which god of thunder and lightning?
4. Jan-Ove Waldner was professionally associated which indoor sport?
5. Which number does the Roman numeral XI represent?
6. Who is the author of the books *The Financial Expert and The Guide*?
7. What's the word?

Set 4

1. Elephant, harp and leopard are all species of which aquatic mammal?
2. Which of these countries is a member of SAARC: Pakistan or Germany?
3. Name the international township and study centre named after Sri Aurobindo Ghose in Puducherry.
4. In India, what happens on a national scale every ten years: census or elections?
5. The name of which planet is an English/German word meaning the 'ground'?
6. Which god, also known as Neelkantha, gave Parashurama his axe: Shiva or Brahma?
7. What's the word?

Set 5

1. In a rainbow, which colour comes between blue and yellow?
2. In *Asterix*, who fell into a cauldron of magic potion when he was a little boy?
3. Which shehnai player was born on 21 March 1916 in Bihar?
4. The duck-billed platypus and the echidna are the only two mammals to do what: lay eggs or fly?
5. What is the opposite of explosion?
6. Before 2006, how many planets were there in the solar system?
7. What's the word?

MATHS AND IQ

1. Amrita finished her work in 4 hours. Ahona finished her work in 400 minutes. Arunita finished her work in 1000 seconds. Who took the maximum time to finish her work?
2. Fill in the blanks with either addition, subtraction, multiplication or division to figure out the correct answer. Go sequentially from left to right without following BODMAS.

11		9		3		46	=	14

3. If the letters of the word ATMOSPHERIC are arranged alphabetically from left to right, which would be the first vowel from the right?
4. What number should logically replace the star in the following series: 4, 9, 25, 49, 121, *, 289?

5. Fill in the blanks with either addition, subtraction, multiplication or division to figure out the correct answer. Go sequentially from left to right without following BODMAS.

6		15		11		2	=	20

VOCABULARY

1. Rearrange the letters of the word 'MEAN' to get what people call you by.
2. Rearrange the letters of the word 'SLIDE' to get the name of a Hindi flim starring Shah Rukh Khan and Preity Zinta. (Hint: Two-word answer in Hindi.)
3. Rearrange the letters of the word 'BAKER' to mean separate into pieces.
4. Read the word 'MINED' backward to get he name of a fabric.
5. Read the word 'WAR' backward to get a word meaning uncooked.

SPEED

1. The Khajuraho temples are in Madhya Pradesh, Uttar Pradesh or Himachal Pradesh?
2. If your mother drinks black coffee, what would be missing from the coffee?
3. The name of which martial art was given by South Korean general Choi Hong-Hi: Tae kwon do, Sumo or Karate?
4. Who played a child actor in the film *Yadoon Ki Baraat:* Salman Khan or Aamir Khan?

5. How many degrees are there in a right angle?
6. Which planet was named after the messenger of the Roman gods?
7. An old-fashioned term for record player is called a gramophone or a turntable?
8. What is a mural painted on?
9. What is basmati a form of?
10. Teen Murti Bhavan in Delhi houses a museum in memory of which former prime minister?

ANSWERS

TAKE YOUR PICK

1. Poodle
2. Meghnad
3. Raja Ravi Varma
4. Asian Games inauguration
5. Amartya
6. Deodar
7. Pasta
8. Ventriloquist
9. Photosynthesis
10. *Koi Mil Gaya*

WHAT'S THE QUESTION

1. What is an antenna?
2. What is an octopus?
3. What does an elephant use its trunk for?
4. In chess, what is the knight also called?
5. What is the composition of air?
6. Which are the letters not used by the World Meteorological Organization in naming Atlantic hurricanes?
7. Who was Dasharatha?
8. The Zambezi River gives its name to which country?
9. What is Ahmedabad?

10. What is actor Rajnikanth's real name?

MIXED BAG

1. East Berlin and West Berlin
2. Eggs
3. Vishwanathan Anand
4. Speed of light in vacuum
5. Mozambique
6. Theodore Roosevelt
7. *Gitanjali* by Rabindranath Tagore
8. Sarojini Naidu
9. Rabindranath Tagore
10. Agra Fort

SPOT THE ANSWER

1. There is no difference
2. Education
3. Kitchen cabinet
4. *101 Dalmatians*
5. Confucius

CONFIDENCE ROUND

1. *The Tempest*
2. Vanilla
3. St Moritz
4. Canada
5. Iodine
6. Euclid

7. Rajasthan
8. Mahatma Gandhi
9. Sri Aurobindo
10. Lucknow

WHAT'S THE WORD

Set 1

1. A.R. Rahman
2. Noodle
3. Kathak
4. Laos
5. Earthworm
6. Tennis
7. ANKLET

Set 2

1. Ravana
2. Australia
3. Charlton Heston
4. Kathak
5. East Bengal and Mohun Bagan
6. Tamil Nadu
7. RACKET

Set 3

1. Larynx
2. Easel
3. Thor
4. Table tennis
5. Eleven

6. R.K. Narayan
7. LETTER

Set 4

1. Seal
2. Pakistan
3. Auroville
4. Census
5. Earth
6. Shiva
7. SPACES

Set 5

1. Green
2. Obelix
3. Bismillah Khan
4. Lay eggs
5. Implosion
6. Nine
7. GOBLIN

MATHS AND IQ

1. Ahona
2.

11	Plus	9	Multiply	3	Minus	46	=	14

3. O
4. 169 (square of prime numbers)
5.

6	Plus	15	Minus	11	Multiply	2	=	20

VOCABULARY

1. NAME
2. *DIL SE*
3. BREAK
4. DENIM
5. RAW

SPEED

1. Madhya Pradesh
2. Milk
3. Tae kwon do
4. Aamir Khan
5. $90°$
6. Mercury
7. Gramophone
8. Wall
9. Rice
10. Jawaharlal Nehru

SET F

1. What is Black Widow a species of?
   a. Spider
   b. Cockroach
   c. Ant

2. A Rest of the World XI vs MCC match played at Lord's in 1987 was which Indian cricketer's last first-class match?
   a. Kapil Dev
   b. Ravi Shastri
   c. Sunil Gavaskar

3. In the Ramayana, who is Rama's sister?
   a. Urmila
   b. Kanta
   c. Shanta

4. In batik method of dyeing, patterned parts are traditionally covered with which substance so that they do not receive colour?
   a. Sugar
   b. Wax
   c. Salt

5. According to Acharya Vinoba Bhave, 'Spirituality + _____ = Sarvodaya'?
   a. Literature
   b. Science
   c. Politics

6. Which is the highest mountain peak outside Asia?
   a. Mount Kilimanjaro
   b. Mount Blanc
   c. Mount Aconcagua

7. Which work by Kalidasa recounts the legend of Rama's ancestors and descendants?
   a. *Meghadutam*
   b. *Vikramorvashi*
   c. *Raghuvansham*

8. Which of these vegetables forms the main ingredient of batata vada?
   a. Cauliflower
   b. Cabbage
   c. Potato

9. Who was the first Indian to win the Ramon Magsaysay Award?
   a. Acharya Vinoba Bhave
   b. Jawaharlal Nehru
   c. S. Radhakrishnan

10. Which fictional character has a boss named M, whose secretary is called Miss Moneypenny?

   a.   Sherlock Holmes
   b.   James Bond
   c.   Clark Kent

WHAT'S THE QUESTION

1. Peachick
2. Sleet
3. The leaves of this plant is used in the body-decorating process known as mehendi.
4. He was the first chief minister of Andhra Pradesh.
5. Raksha, a she-wolf, took care of him.
6. This country was known as Ceylon.
7. This word is a blend of the words smoke and fog.
8. This ruler gave up warfare despite being victorious in the Kalinga War.
9. It is the deepest lake in the world.
10. Samta Sthal

MIXED BAG

1. If you visited the Karni Mata Temple at Bikaner in Rajasthan, which animal or animals would you see being worshipped?
2. Which town was known as Vatapi in ancient times and was the first capital of the Chalukya kings?
3. Which is the only living species in the genus Struthio?
4. Crisscross words is an earlier version of which board game?
5. Shanti Van is the samadhi of which prime minister of India?

6. In the 1830s, what was marketed in the United States as Dr Miles's compound extract of tomato?

7. 'Yours is the Earth and everything that's in it, And—which is more—you'll be a Man, my son!' These are the last few lines of which poem?

8. Which word did Van Helmont invent to describe substances 'far more subtle or fine...than a vapour, mist, or distilled oiliness, although...many times thicker than air'?

9. Which overseas territory of the United Kingdom is also known as the Malvinas Islands?

10. Which famous Steven Spielberg film began with a woman being killed by a great white shark?

SPOT THE ANSWER

1. Which system of medical practice is based on 'like cures like'?
   a. Allopathy
   b. Acupuncture
   c. Homeopathy

2. What would you do with a tom yum?
   a. Play with it. It is a yo-yo.
   b. Climb it. It is the highest mountain in China.
   c. Eat it. It is a Thai soup.

3. Which tree did Tipu Sultan declare as a royal tree and monopolized its trade in 1792?
   a. Banyan
   b. Mango

   c.   Sandalwood

4. What is vellum, used for writing or printing on, made from?
   a.   Wood from the banyan tree
   b.   Animal skins
   c.   Wood from the eucalyptus tree

5. The name of which disease comes from a word in the Kimakonde language, meaning 'to become contorted', and describes the stooped appearance of sufferers?
   a.   Malaria
   b.   Chikungunya
   c.   Dengue

CONFIDENCE ROUND

1. In Hindu mythology, who is also known as Ganapati?
2. How many wisdom teeth do adult humans usually have: three, four, five or six?
3. Which colour is associated with the Dutch royal family: magenta or orange?
4. What did Omar Khayyam write: *Rubbaiyat* or *Shahmat*?
5. Which game in India is normally associated with 'tip cat': gilli danda or ludo?
6. Which is closer to Delhi: Bhopal or Hyderabad?
7. How many colours does the South African flag display?
8. Which novel by Emily Bronte revolves around Heathcliff and Edgar Linton?

9. Which is a positive word: Zindabad or Murdabad?
10. What is the principal ingredient of omelettes?

WHAT'S THE WORD

Set 1

1. In *Asterix*, who is also known as Troubadix in German?
2. What would you call a medium-sized sailing boat equipped for cruising or racing: coracle or yacht?
3. Which former cricketer was nicknamed 'Big C' or 'Hubert'?
4. If Lord Shiva's abode is Kailash, who stays at Vaikuntha: Lord Ganesha or Lord Vishnu?
5. What would you call an electronic version of a printed book?
6. Koodiyattam, performed by the Chakyar of Kerala, is the only surviving theatre form in which language?
7. What's the word?

Set 2

1. Which legendary British king was the son of King Uther Pendragon?
2. Hing Kabuli Sufaid and Hing Lal are the two main varieties of asafoetida or fenugreek?
3. What does 'ra' in the abbreviation Radar stand for?
4. What is the official language of Egypt: Urdu or Arabic?
5. In terms of transport, what connects an autorickshaw and a tricycle: three wheels or three engines?
6. Which key on a standard keyboard is used to perform

various functions, such as executing a command or selecting options on a menu?

7. What's the word?

Set 3

1. *Open: An Autobiography* is written by which professional tennis player?
2. The name of which Union Territory means 'hundred thousand islands' in Sanskrit?
3. If you visited Arjuna's Penance, which temple town would you be in?
4. What is the name of the cat in the animated television series *Oggy and the Cockroaches*?
5. Which river in Central India was called Namade by the 2nd century Greek geographer Ptolemy?
6. Iraq was once the world's largest producer of date or coconut?
7. What's the word?

Set 4

1. What type of a fruit is an alphonso?
2. Which 1996 English film starring Arnold Schwarzenegger shares its name with a stationary item?
3. In English grammar, which word comes from a Latin word meaning 'name': phrase or noun?
4. Which cartoon duo's first cartoon together was called *Puss Gets the Boot*?
5. The name of which viscous liquid comes from the Latin word *oleum*?
6. Which animal is the zodiac sign of the constellation Aries?

7. What's the word?

Set 5

1. Which Indian did Han Jian lose to at the 1981 badminton World Cup final?
2. Which word describes a hundred thousand?
3. Which film actor connects *Lal Badshah*, *Agneepath* and *Sooryavansham*?
4. Which of these is an amphibian: newt or turtle?
5. What is the hard glossy substance that covers the crown of a tooth called?
6. M. Karunanidhi was the chief minister of which state in India?
7. What's the word?

MATHS AND IQ

1. At a meeting there were 1000 men. If 26 men out of every 50 wore black ties, how many did not wear black ties?
2. Fill in the blanks with either addition, subtraction, multiplication or division to figure out the correct answer. Go sequentially from left to right without following BODMAS.

8		5		4		32	=	20

3. One evening, just before sunset, Nisha and Nishant were talking to each other, face to face, on Nisha's terrace. If Nishant's shadow was exactly to the left of Nisha, which direction was Nishant facing?
4. Fill in the blanks with either addition, subtraction, multiplication or division to figure out the correct

answer. Go sequentially from left to right without following BODMAS.

60		12		3		23	=	25

5. Which 3 letters will logically complete the series: ACF, GIL, MOR, _____ ?

VOCABULARY

1. Rearrange the letters of the word 'ELBOW' to get the opposite of above.
2. Rearrange the letters of the word 'VOTES' to get a kitchen appliance used for heating.
3. Rearrange the letters of the word 'BAKE' to mean a bird's body part.
4. Read the word 'PETS' backward to mean an act of walking.
5. Read the word 'TEN' backward to get the name of a material used for catching fish.

SPEED

1. In which European country did Charles Lindbergh complete his transatlantic flight?
2. Exactly when did India get independence: midnight of August 14 or midnight of August 15?
3. Which is Delhi's best known observatory?
4. Which festival is celebrated on the same day as Narali Poornima or Coconut Day is in Maharashtra?
5. Is a kilogram more or less than a pound?
6. Was Athena a Greek goddess or a Roman goddess?

7. In which story would you find the Marquis of Carabas?

8. What four-letter word best describes the stitching on a cricket ball?

9. Who usually gets admitted into maternity wards: mummies, daddies or grandpas?

10. What was Phantom also known as: Mr Walker or Mr Runner?

ANSWERS

TAKE YOUR PICK

1. Spider
2. Sunil Gavaskar
3. Shanta
4. Wax
5. Science
6. Mount Aconcagua
7. *Raghuvansham*
8. Potato
9. Acharya Vinoba Bhave
10. James Bond

WHAT'S THE QUESTION

1. What is the baby of a peafowl called?
2. In Great Britain, what is the name for a wet mixture of snow and rain?
3. What is henna?
4. What was N. Sanjiva Reddy?
5. Who was Mowgli?
6. What is Sri Lanka?
7. What is smog?
8. Who was Ashoka?
9. Which is Lake Baikal?
10. What is the name of the samadhi of former Deputy

Prime Minister Jagjivan Ram?

MIXED BAG

1. Rats
2. Badami
3. Ostrich
4. Scrabble
5. Jawaharlal Nehru
6. Ketchup
7. *If* (by Rudyard Kipling)
8. Gas
9. Falkland Islands
10. *Jaws*

SPOT THE ANSWER

1. Homeopathy
2. Eat it. It is a Thai soup.
3. Sandalwood
4. Animal skins
5. Chikungunya

CONFIDENCE ROUND

1. Ganesha
2. Four
3. Orange
4. *Rubbaiyat*
5. Gilli danda
6. Bhopal

7. Six
8. *Wuthering Heights*
9. Zindabad
10. Egg

WHAT'S THE WORD

Set 1

1. Cacofonix
2. Yacht
3. Clive Lloyd
4. Lord Vishnu
5. E-book
6. Sanskrit
7. CYCLES

Set 2

1. King Arthur
2. Asafoetida
3. Radio
4. Arabic
5. Three wheels
6. Enter
7. KARATE

Set 3

1. Andre Agassi
2. Lakshadweep
3. Mahabalipuram in Tamil Nadu
4. Oggy
5. Narmada

6. Date
7. ALMOND

Set 4

1. Mango
2. *Eraser*
3. Noun
4. *Tom and Jerry* (Initially named Jasper and Jinx, only Tom was identified as Jasper onscreen.)
5. Oil
6. Ram
7. MENTOR

Set 5

1. Prakash Padukone
2. Lakh
3. Amitabh Bachchan
4. Newt
5. Enamel
6. Tamil Nadu
7. PLANET

MATHS AND IQ

1. 480

2.
8	Plus	5	Multiply	4	Minus	32	=	20

3. North

4.
60	Divide	12	Minus	3	Plus	23	=	25

5. SUX

VOCABULARY

1. BELOW
2. STOVE
3. BEAK
4. STEP
5. NET

SPEED

1. France
2. The midnight of August 14
3. Jantar Mantar
4. Raksha Bandhan
5. More. One kilogram is equal to 2.2 pounds.
6. Greek. Minerva is her Roman equivalnet.
7. *Puss in Boots*
8. Seam
9. Mummies
10. Mr Walker

SET G

1. In International women's cricket, the first Test match won by India was against which team?
   a. England
   b. Australia
   c. West Indies

2. In Karnataka, a yakshagana performance starts and ends with a prayer to which god?
   a. Ganesha
   b. Rama
   c. Indra

3. What did Louis Braille lose while he was playing in his father's shop at the age of three?
   a. His teeth
   b. His sight
   c. His speech

4. Which river rises in the Black Forest mountains of western Germany and flows to the Black Sea?
   a. Danube
   b. Volga
   c. Rhine

5. In Hindu mythology, who is the god of death?
   a. Yama
   b. Indra
   c. Surya

6. Which famous English author was born in 1903 in Motihari in Bihar?
   a. George Orwell
   b. Rudyard Kipling
   c. Ruskin Bond

7. What is a tandoor oven traditionally made of?
   a. Wood
   b. Metal
   c. Clay

8. Who is a couch potato?
   a. A person who spends a great deal of time eating potato chips
   b. A person who spends a great deal of time watching television and exercising
   c. A person who spends a great deal of time watching television and almost no time exercising

9. What does 'M' in MRI stand for?
   a. Musical
   b. Magnetic
   c. Mirror

10. Which musician played the role of Inder Lal in the 1983 film *Heat and Dust*?

a. U Srinivas
b. Zakir Hussain
c. Shiv Kumar Sharma

WHAT'S THE QUESTION

1. He wrote the book *Curries and Other Indian Dishes*.
2. Right Faith, Right Knowledge, Right Conduct
3. It is called Al-Bahr Al-Ahmar in Arabic.
4. In 1973, after eighteen years in exile, he was re-elected president of Argentina.
5. Baba Buddha was the first keeper of this religious book.
6. Sir Ronald Ross discovered it within the Anopheles mosquito in 1897.
7. It is usually divided into the Palaeolithic, Mesolithic and Neolithic Ages.
8. Their celebration is called a jamboree.
9. This unit of length, often used in reference to depth of water, is equal to six feet.
10. He was exiled on the island of Elba in 1814–15.

MIXED BAG

1. If Scotland is known for its bagpipes, what musical instrument is the national symbol of Ireland?
2. The hammer, anvil and stirrup are bones in which organ of the human body?
3. Which mountain peak is locally called Dapsang or Chogori?
4. Which national park is situated 14 km from Sawai

Madhopur and derives its name from the fort situated within its precincts?

5. Who built the famous Buland Darwaza to commemorate his victory in Gujarat?

6. In the 1984 parliamentary elections, which famous person did Madhavrao Scindia defeat in the Gwalior constituency?

7. What nickname is common to former cricketer Venkatapathy Raju and former tennis player Ken Rosewall?

8. What were sometimes called 'dissected maps' and were used to teach geography in England?

9. United States Patent No. 174465, issued in 1876, and recognized as the 'most valuable patent' was for what?

10. Who was the first actor to appear on the cover of *Time* magazine?

SPOT THE ANSWER

1. Which of these is another name for tea ceremony in Japan?
   a. Origami
   b. Bonsai
   c. Sado

2. In which novel by Charles Dickens would you meet Agnes Wickfield, James Steerforth and Clara Peggotty?
   a. *A Christmas Carol*
   b. *Oliver Twist*
   c. *David Copperfield*

3. How many milligrams make a kilogram?
   a. One thousand
   b. Ten thousand
   c. One million

4. With which sport would you associate the jumping style called Fosbury Flop?
   a. Long jump
   b. High jump
   c. Pole vault

5. Who among these was the son of a Pandava?
   a. Jatasura
   b. Ravana
   c. Ghatotkacha

CONFIDENCE ROUND

1. A person who studies rocks is called a rock star: serious or joking?
2. How much is two score and seven?
3. The opposite of manual is annual or automatic?
4. In I.C.S.E. and C.B.S.E., what does 'E' stand for?
5. Which affectionate term means zero in tennis?
6. In which continent is Spain located?
7. What is the main liquid in the English Channel?
8. Rajaraja I belonged to which dynasty: Cholas, Chalukyas or Hoysalas?
9. After which leader is the international airport of New Delhi named?
10. Is Patna on the Ganga or the Brahmaputra?

WHAT'S THE WORD

Set 1

1. Complete the name of this book by Roald Dahl: *Charlie and the ____ Factory*?
2. In which state of India is the Mount Abu Sanctuary located?
3. Which character did Amitabh Bachchan play in the film *Amar Akbar Anthony*?
4. Which unit of linear measure equal to 3 feet?
5. What is the study and treatment of tumours called?
6. The Empire State building in the US is named after the nickname of which state?
7. What's the word?

Set 2

1. Who gave the name Nivedita to Margaret Elizabeth Noble: Swami Vivekananda or Subhas Chandra Bose?
2. The name of which microscopic organism comes from the Sanskrit word *yas* which means 'to seethe or boil'?
3. According to mythology, what is the name of Krishna's chakra?
4. Siberian, Sumatran and Bengal are species of which animal?
5. Which disease is named after a river in the Democratic Republic of Congo (Zaire), near which the disease was first observed?
6. Which painter directed the film *Meenaxi: A Tale of Three Cities*?

7. What's the word?

Set 3

1. What is usually added to bread to make it rise?
2. Which is the home ground of the Bengal cricket team?
3. The name of which slow-growing plant comes from the Greek word *leikhēn*?
4. The museum, Madam Tussauds, is located in which city of England?
5. Which branch of medicine is concerned with the study and treatment of disorders and diseases of the eye?
6. Warszawa is another name of which city?
7. What's the word?

Set 4

1. In anthropology, which term is used to describe a member of any human group whose adult males grow to less than 150 cm (59 inches) in average height?
2. The name of which gemstone is said to be based on the Sanskrit word *upala* meaning 'precious stone'?
3. Canines and wisdom are types of what?
4. Amitabh Bachchan plays the role of the father in the film *Mahaan*. Who plays the role of his twin sons?
5. Which popular story by Robert Louis Stevenson was originally titled *The Sea Cook*?
6. Which is the largest city of Norway?
7. What's the word?

Set 5

1. In Hindi, it is called *bhaloo*. What is it called in English?

2. Who is the first prime minister since Pandit Jawaharlal Nehru to have become prime minister of India with two successive mandates?
3. Nocturnal animals are active during the day or night?
4. In the medical condition, jaundice, what colour does the skin or the whites of the eyes become?
5. Two Indian states have the same initials and end with the same seven-letter words. Name them.
6. Peter Pan fell out of his carriage and was taken to which fictional land?
7. What's the word?

MATHS AND IQ

1. Which number will logically replace the # sign in the following series: 4, 13, #, 193, 769, 3073?
2. Fill in the blanks with either addition, subtraction, multiplication or division to figure out the correct answer. Go sequentially from left to right without following BODMAS.

9		3		53		4	=	20

3. If today is Thursday, which day would be the day after tomorrow of the day before yesterday?
4. Fill in the blanks with either addition, subtraction, multiplication or division to figure out the correct answer. Go sequentially from left to right without following BODMAS.

45		30		5		3	=	25

5. Which letter should be added to RIDE to get the word denoting a group of lions?

VOCABULARY

1. Rearrange the letters of the word 'SHELF' to mean something that the human body is made up of.
2. Rearrange the letters of the word 'CHEATER' to mean a person who provides education for students.
3. Rearrange the letters of the word 'LIFE' to get a folder or box for holding loose papers together.
4. Read the word 'KNITS' backward to mean something that emits a strong foul odour.
5. Read the word 'STAR' backward to get the name of a rodent.

SPEED

1. Nagaland is on the border of Bangladesh, Myanmar or Pakistan?
2. Plumage is the correct term for which part of a bird?
3. What is the capital of the Tibet Autonomous Region, southwestern China?
4. How many metres are there in 300 centimetres?
5. Which Indian-born footballer played for Bury Football Club in 2001?
6. The famous Pragati Maidan is situated in Bangalore, New Delhi or Chandigarh?
7. The recipients of the Victoria Cross are entitled to add which two letters after their name?
8. The inside of a spoon is convex or concave?
9. Who starred in the 1981 film *Umrao Jaan*: Rekha or Rakhee?
10. Which historical site is in present-day Pakistan: Taxila or Pataliputra?

ANSWERS

TAKE YOUR PICK

1. West Indies
2. Ganesha
3. His sight
4. Danube
5. Yama
6. George Orwell
7. Clay
8. A person who spends a great deal of time watching television and almost no time exercising.
9. Magnetic
10. Zakir Hussain

WHAT'S THE QUESTION

1. Who is Mulk Raj Anand?
2. What are the three jewels of Jainism?
3. What is the Arabic name of Red Sea?
4. Who was Juan Perón?
5. In 1604, who was appointed as the first keeper of the Guru Granth Sahib?
6. Who discovered the presence of the malarial parasite in the *Anopheles* mosquito?
7. Into what periods is the Stone Age divided?
8. What do you call a large rally by a group of Scouts?

9. What is a fathom?
10. Name the island on which Napoleon was exiled.

MIXED BAG

1. Harp
2. Ear
3. K2
4. Ranthambore National Park
5. Akbar
6. Atal Bihari Vajpayee
7. Muscles
8. Jigsaw puzzles
9. Telephone
10. Charlie Chaplin

SPOT THE ANSWER

1. Sado
2. *David Copperfield*
3. One million
4. High jump
5. Ghatotkacha

CONFIDENCE ROUND

1. Joking
2. 47
3. Automatic
4. Education
5. Love

6. Europe
7. Water
8. Cholas
9. Indira Gandhi
10. Ganga

WHAT'S THE WORD

Set 1

1. *Chocolate*
2. Rajasthan
3. Anthony Gonsalves
4. Yard
5. Oncology
5. New York
7. CRAYON

Set 2

1. Swami Vivekananda
2. Yeast
3. Sudarshan
4. Tiger
5. Ebola
6. M.F. Hussain
7. SYSTEM

Set 3

1. Yeast
2. Eden Gardens
3. Lichen
4. London

5. Ophthalmology
6. Warsaw
7. YELLOW

Set 4

1. Pygmy
2. Opal
3. Teeth
4. Amitabh Bachchan (He had a triple role.)
5. *Treasure Island*
6. Oslo
7. POTATO

Set 5

1. Bear
2. Atal Bihari Vajpayee
3. Night
4. Yellow
5. Andhra Pradesh and Arunachal Pradesh
6. Never Never Land
7. BANYAN

MATHS AND IQ

1. 49 (Each number in the series is the preceding number multiplied by 4 and then decreased by 3.)

2.

9	Multiply	3	Plus	53	Divide	4	=	20

3. Thursday

4.

45	Minus	30	Multiply	5	Divide	3	=	25

5. P

VOCABULARY

1. FLESH
2. TEACHER
3. FILE
4. STINK
5. RATS

SPEED

1. Myanmar
2. Feathers
3. Lhasa
4. Three
5. Bhaichung Bhutia
6. New Delhi
7. V.C.
8. Concave
9. Rekha
10. Taxila

SET H

TAKE YOUR PICK

1. Which of these animals holds the record for having the largest brain in the world?
   a. Sperm whale
   b. Elephant
   c. Giraffe

2. Which of these cricket umpires also acted as a referee in a Football World Cup qualifying match?
   a. Steve Bucknor
   b. David Shepherd
   c. Dickie Bird

3. In ancient Rome, the warning 'cave canem' was meant for people to beware of which animal?
   a. Dog
   b. Cat
   c. Eagle

4. Which art form of Persia was introduced in Rajasthan under the patronage of Maharaja Sawai Ram Singhji?
   a. Batik
   b. Filigree
   c. Blue pottery

5. Which Indian state was known as the Lushai Hills District of Assam before it was renamed in 1954?
   a. Meghalaya
   b. Mizoram
   c. Nagaland

6. In Hindu mythology, who received the 'Brahma Sirastra' for saving Dronacharya's life?
   a. Bhima
   b. Arjuna
   c. Duryodhana

7. In which book would you come across the characters Mercedes and Abbe Faria?
   a. *Oliver Twist*
   b. *The Count of Monte Cristo*
   c. *Gulliver's Travels*

8. Which fruit was referred to as love apple by the French?
   a. Apple
   b. Cherry
   c. Tomato

9. What would a graphologist study?
   a. Handwriting
   b. Gemstones
   c. Birds

10. In which film would you meet these seven children: Liesl, Louisa, Friedrich, Kurt, Brigitta, Marta and Gretl?

a. *Rapunzel*
b. *Mary Poppins*
c. *The Sound of Music*

WHAT'S THE QUESTION

1. Snowline
2. Moa is an extinct bird that was native to this country.
3. The first UN Secretary-General from Africa.
4. This dynasty was founded by a Chagatai Turkic prince named Babur.
5. Spun sugar on a stick
6. The flag of this country features the map of the country above two olive branches.
7. Trapezium
8. Yeti
9. Baht
10. In Hindi, it is known as *adrak*.

MIXED BAG

1. What is common to simple, greenstick, Pott's or impacted?
2. The famous Sun Temple of Modhera is located in which state?
3. Which observatory did Sawai Jai Singh build at Delhi, Jaipur, Varanasi, Mathura and Ujjain?
4. A hinny is a hybrid offspring of which two animals?
5. Set in the 1950s, which novel revolves around the fortunes of four families: the Mehras, the Kapoors, the Khans and the Chatterjis?

6. What was the code name of the Indian operation in the Kargil war?

7. Which sportsman was once nicknamed 'The Louisville Lip'?

8. What does OMOV mean in terms of voting in many countries?

9. What part of a car engine is called a muffler in the US?

10. Who received the National Film Award for his debut role as a child artist in the film *Mera Naam Joker*?

SPOT THE ANSWER

1. Putrajaya is a city in…
   a. Malaysia
   b. Brunei
   c. Turkey

2. In which novel by Charles Dickens was the main character haunted by three spirits who took him to the past, present and future?
   a. *A Christmas Carol*
   b. *Oliver Twist*
   c. *David Copperfield*

3. The flightless bird rhea is native to which continent?
   a. Africa
   b. South America
   c. Asia

4. Which is the human body's biggest consumer

of oxygen and the first organ to suffer if there is a shortage?

a. Brain
b. Kidney
c. Heart

5. In 1813–14, Ranjit Singh, the king of Punjab, brought what back to India?
    a. Peacock Throne
    b. Koh-i-noor diamond
    c. His title

CONFIDENCE ROUND

1. Which is not a vertebrate: a python or a snail?
2. Maharashtra is the most populous state in India: serious or joking?
3. Which superhero's relative said: 'With great power comes great responsibility'?
4. What is a greenhouse made of?
5. What does the red circle on the Japanese flag represent?
6. Cinderella's coach was made from a guava: serious or joking?
7. Alphabetically, which country's capital comes earlier: Bangladesh or India?
8. In which sport is there a scrum: rugby or hockey?
9. Which water body is associated with the word 'Persian': bay or gulf?
10. Which epidemic in the 1300s in Europe got its name from the black spots on the victims' bodies?

WHAT'S THE WORD

Set 1

1. The name of which desert is derived from *t'hul*, the general term for sand ridges?
2. Which gas protects the Earth from harmful ultraviolet rays?
3. What does 'U' in USB stand for?
4. Complete the proverb: Curiosity killed the _____.
5. Which is the study of the human skeleton: anatomy or astronomy?
6. By which name was the empress Mihr-un-nisa better known?
7. What's the word?

Set 2

1. The scientific name of which tree is *Azadirachta indica*: neem or peepal?
2. Kampala is the largest city of which country?
3. How is peppermint camphor better known?
4. Which word means 'One of the Majority' in Russian: Menshevik or Bolshevik?
5. What is the inflammation of the brain, caused by infection or an allergic reaction called: Encephalitis or Sinus?
6. Remy, a young rat, dreams of becoming a renowned French chef in which 2007 animated film?
7. What's the word?

Set 3

1. The fourteen coaches of which luxury train are named after former Rajput states?
2. The name of which country comes from the Equator which divides it unequally?
3. Which famous Kathak dancer founded a dance school named Kalashram: Pandit Birju Maharaj or Uday Shankar?
4. In Greek mythology, who opened a box and set free all evils?
5. As a department in a hospital, what does 'E' in the abbreviation ENT stand for?
6. The name of which animal comes from the Greek words for 'nose' and 'horn'?
7. What's the word?

Set 4

1. What is a flat paper container with a sealable flap, used to enclose a letter called?
2. Which independent emirate is located on the west coast of the Persian Gulf?
3. In the Ramayana, who was Lakshmana's wife?
4. Who played the female lead in the film *Aur Pyaar Ho Gaya*?
5. Which former Indian princely state lies between Assam, Mizoram and Bangladesh?
6. If kangaroo is one of the animals in the Australian Coat of Arms, which is the other?
7. What's the word?

Set 5

1. Who has been India's longest-serving prime minister?
2. If Vishakhapatnam is in Andhra Pradesh, in which state is Vijayawada?
3. Which famous monument is in Mumbai: Gateway of India or India Gate?
4. The original logo of which organisation was created by a team of designers, led by Oliver Lincoln Lundquist, in 1945?
5. In computers, what does 'A' in the abbreviation CAD stand for?
6. What is the correct geometric name of an equilateral parallelogram?
7. What's the word?

MATHS AND IQ

1. In the word RECTANGULAR, how many letters appear in the same positions as they do in the alphabet?
2. Fill in the blanks with either addition, subtraction, multiplication or division to figure out the correct answer. Go sequentially from left to right without following BODMAS.

8		6		12		1	=	5

3. I am a number between 20 and 40. One of my digits is half the other. The product of the digits is twice the sum of the digits. Which number am I?
4. Which is the odd one and why?
   PIUTEJR, TUARSN, PMLUATNI, NEENPUT

5. Fill in the blanks with either addition, subtraction, multiplication or division to figure out the correct answer. Go sequentially from left to right without following BODMAS.

15		4		20		22	=	25

VOCABULARY

1. Rearrange the letters of the word 'CAUSE' to get a liquid substance served with food.
2. Rearrange the letters of the word 'MARINE' to get a word meaning continue to exist.
3. Rearrange the letters of the word 'HEART' to get the name of a planet.
4. Rearrange the letters of the word 'CHARM' to get the name of a month.
5. Read the word 'GEL' backward to get a part of the human body.

SPEED

1. Is tungsten a gas, liquid or metal?
2. On what surface is the French Open tennis tournament played?
3. Who is the first woman prime minister of India?
4. Which river flows through Washington DC?
5. Humayun was Akbar's father, grandfather or uncle?
6. What would you call a person who composes dance sequences in a film?
7. If Richie Rich applied for a passport, what would he write under the surname column?

8. Karma Bhoomi is the memorial to Shankar Dayal Sharma or Jagjivan Ram?
9. What is the official language of Mexico?
10. What are you doing if your lachrymal glands are secreting liquid?

ANSWERS

TAKE YOUR PICK

1. Sperm whale
2. Steve Bucknor
3. Dog
4. Blue pottery
5. Mizoram
6. Arjuna
7. *The Count of Monte Cristo*
8. Tomato
9. Handwriting
10. *The Sound of Music*

WHAT'S THE QUESTION

1. What do you call the line on high mountains above which snow never melts?
2. What is New Zealand?
3. Who is Boutros Boutros-Ghali?
4. Who founded the Mughal dynasty?
5. What is candyfloss?
6. What is the flag of Cyprus?
7. In Great Britain, what do you call a four-sided plane figure with one pair of parallel sides?
8. What is another name for the Abominable Snowman?
9. What is the currency of Thailand?

10. What is ginger called in Hindi?

MIXED BAG

1. They are different types of fractures.
2. Gujarat
3. Jantar Mantar
4. A male horse and a female donkey
5. *A Suitable Boy* by Vikram Seth
6. Operation Vijay
7. Muhammad Ali
8. One Member One Vote
9. Silencer
10. Rishi Kapoor

SPOT THE ANSWER

1. Malaysia
2. *A Christmas Carol*. In the book, the miser Ebenezer Scrooge is visited by the Ghosts of Christmas Past, Present, and Yet to Come.
3. South America
4. Brain
5. Koh-i-noor diamond

CONFIDENCE ROUND

1. Snail
2. Joking. India's most populous state is Uttar Pradesh as on 23rd June, 2014.
3. Spider-Man

4. Glass
5. The sun
6. Joking; it was made from a pumpkin
7. Bangladesh
8. Rugby
9. Gulf
10. Black Death

WHAT'S THE WORD

Set 1

1. Thar
2. Ozone
3. Universal
4. Cat
5. Anatomy
6. Nur Jahan
7. TOUCAN

Set 2

1. Neem
2. Uganda
3. Menthol
4. Bolshevik
5. Encephalitis
6. *Ratatouille*
7. NUMBER

Set 3

1. Palace on Wheels
2. Ecuador

3. Pandit Birju Maharaj; Kalashram is in New Delhi
4. Pandora
5. Ear
6. Rhinoceros
7. PEPPER

Set 4

1. Envelope
2. Qatar
3. Urmila
4. Aishwarya Rai
5. Tripura
6. Emu
7. EQUATE

Set 5

1. Jawaharlal Nehru
2. Andhra Pradesh
3. Gateway of India
4. United Nations
5. Aided
6. Rhombus
7. JAGUAR

MATHS AND IQ

1. 2 (C, G)
2.

8	Multiply	6	Divide	12	Plus	1	=	5

3. 36
4. PMLUATNI (PLATINUM), others are names of planets: JUPITER, SATURN, NEPTUNE

5. | 15 | Multiply | 4 | Divide | 20 | Plus | 22 | = | 25 |
|---|---|---|---|---|---|---|---|---|

VOCABULARY

1. SAUCE
2. REMAIN
3. EARTH
4. MARCH
5. LEG

SPEED

1. Metal
2. Clay
3. Indira Gandhi
4. Potomac River
5. Father
6. Choreographer
7. Rich
8. Shankar Dayal Sharma
9. Spanish
10. Crying

SET I

TAKE YOUR PICK

1. Which creature is considered the most intelligent of all invertebrates?
   a. Starfish
   b. Box Jellyfish
   c. Common octopus

2. Of which international sporting event were Kaz, Ato and Nik mascots?
   a. FIFA World Cup 2002
   b. Winter Olympics 2002
   c. Summer Olympics 2000

3. With which food item does the legendary king, who presides over the carnival in Goa, share his name?
   a. Momo
   b. Thukpa
   c. Sushi

4. The oldest capital of which south Indian dynasty was Uraiyur (now Tirachirapalli)?
   a. Chola
   b. Pandya
   c. Chera

5. In which of these states are you most likely to find the Chota Nagpur plateau?
   a. Tamil Nadu
   b. Jharkhand
   c. Maharashtra

6. On which musical instrument would you find 'syahi'?
   a. Sitar
   b. Tabla
   c. Flute

7. The treatise Tolkappiyam is the earliest existing theoretical work in which Indian language?
   a. Marathi
   b. Gujarati
   c. Tamil

8. In India, with which food item was Operation Flood associated?
   a. Sugar
   b. Milk
   c. Tea

9. The logo of which organization features a burning candle wrapped in barbed wire?
   a. Amnesty International
   b. Missionaries of Charity
   c. World Health Organization

10. In Hindu mythology, whose eighth son was named Devavrata?

a. Ambika
b. Ganga
c. Ambalika

WHAT'S THE QUESTION

1. The name of this animal means 'giraffe-necked' in the Somali language.
2. Another name for asteroids
3. This politician's father was the chief minister of Jammu and Kashmir between 1996 and 2002.
4. Starchy substance obtained from cassava roots
5. US portrait painter known for his dot-and-dash code system
6. In Hindu mythology, Ganga and Satyavati were his two wives.
7. A doughnut-shaped fried snack from southern India
8. Jungle Book's 'great grey lone wolf'
9. In India, it is also known as the 'Car Festival'.
10. It appeared on the Chinese flag till 1911.

MIXED BAG

1. With which organ of the human body would you associate the word 'renal'?
2. Who was the first recipient of the Dadasaheb Phalke Award?
3. *The Story of My Life* is the autobiography of the first non-Congress prime minister of independent India. Name him.
4. Which Asian country in the Pacific Ocean is made up

of 7,107 islands, the largest of them being Luzon?

5. Which bird has the largest eye of any land animal?

6. Name the mausoleum of Muhammad Adil Shah which distinctly echoes even the faintest whisper over ten times.

7. I have a brother named Mycroft. My character is based on the surgeon Dr Joseph Bell. I was created by Sir Arthur Conan Doyle. Who am I?

8. The name of which Indian percussion instrument literally means 'made of clay'?

9. What was the code name of the secret project to develop atomic bombs during World War II in the US?

10. Which German football player is credited with inventing the 'attacking sweeper' position?

SPOT THE ANSWER

1. In India, which of these notes does not have the special feature that helps the visually impaired to identify the denomination?
   a. ₹10
   b. ₹20
   c. ₹50

2. The name of which of these cities literally means 'the city of cut-stone'?
   a. Nalanda
   b. Kalinga
   c. Taxila

3. From the tears of which god is the rudraksha tree believed to have originated?
   a. Vishnu
   b. Shiva
   c. Brahma

4. In 1933, what was created by Hermann Goring from the political and espionage units of the police of the German state of Prussia?
   a. CIA
   b. Gestapo
   c. Buchenwald

5. The 'Srikalahasti' and 'Machalipatnam' styles of Kalamkari art originated in…
   a. West Bengal
   b. Andhra Pradesh
   c. Odisha

CONFIDENCE ROUND

1. Which director is common to the films *Mr India* and *Bandit Queen*?
2. What kind of birds provided early airmail services?
3. A cube has: four, six or eight faces?
4. A hinge joint joins your arm and shoulder: serious or joking?
5. Is Cherrapunji in Assam or Meghalaya?
6. Which is the first month in the Saka calendar?
7. In the Bible, who built an ark to save the animals?
8. Expand the acronym UFO.

9. The name of which character is a synonym for a miser: Scrooge or Fagin?
10. In a dictionary, what comes first: snow or sleet?

WHAT'S THE WORD

Set 1

1. Which city, located in Jharkhand, is considered to be India's first planned industrial city?
2. Around which part of your body would you wear a bajuband?
3. The superhero Batman is also known as the 'Caped Crusader' or 'the Man of Steel'?
4. Which word literally means 'empty orchestra' in Japanese?
5. Which short novel, one of the outstanding Christmas stories of modern literature, by Charles Dickens was originally published in 1843?
6. Which of these is located in Europe: Lebanon or Latvia?
7. What's the word?

Set 2

1. Pamulaparti Venkata were the first names of which prime minister of India?
2. Which actor connects the films : *Dil*, *Mann* and *Ghulam*: Aamir Khan or Salman Khan?
3. Who was referred to by the title Admiral of the Seven Seas?
4. What is the Indian variant of ice cream that is served with faluda?

5. What is the tidal mouth of a large river, where the tide meets the stream called?

6. Who does the cartoon cat Sylvester always try to catch and eat?

7. What's the word?

Set 3

1. How many years did Rip Van Winkle sleep?

2. Originally from Africa, which vegetable is also known as *bhindi* or lady's finger: okra or gumbo?

3. After which goddess in Norse mythology is Friday named?

4. A badger's burrow is called a sett. What do you call a hare's lair?

5. Aural polyps affect which organ of the human body?

6. Which keyboard key is commonly used to move the cursor to the bottom of the screen or file?

7. What's the word?

Set 4

1. Which actress became Miss India in 1984?

2. Grandmaster is the highest classification for a chess player. What is the classification immediately below it?

3. Sinus cavities are located in the bony skull of which sense organ?

4. Which spice is shaped like a bulb: garlic or ginger?

5. Which famous artist was known as 'Il Florentine' because he lived near Florence?

6. In which language did R.K. Narayan write his first novel?

7. What's the word?

Set 5

1. Which mythical animal appears on the flag of Bhutan?
2. What is the traditional Japanese art of paper folding called?
3. Which was established later: United Nations or League of Nations?
4. Which Mughal emperor was Umar Sheikh Mirza's son?
5. In the Ramayana, which city did Hanuman burn with the fire from his tail?
6. What is the point on the Earth's surface vertically above the focus of an earthquake called?
7. What's the word?

MATHS AND IQ

1. If A=1, B=2, C=3 and so on, what is the sum total of the consonants in the word MARCH?
2. Fill in the blanks with either addition, subtraction, multiplication or division to figure out the correct answer. Go sequentially from left to right without following BODMAS.

4		2		9		6	=	5

3. In a class, Geeta is sitting on Mita's left. Sita is sitting on Mita's right. Rita is sitting on Geeta's left. Arpita is sitting on Rita's left. Who is sitting on Geeta's right?
4. Fill in the blanks with either addition, subtraction, multiplication or division to figure out the correct answer. Go sequentially from left to right without following BODMAS.

14		2		9		2	=	32

5. Which number will logically replace the # sign in the following series? 3, 6, 18, 72, #

VOCABULARY

1. Rearrange the letters of the word 'PEA' to get the name of a primate without a tail.
2. Rearrange the letters of the word 'PRESENT' to mean a large snake.
3. Rearrange the letters of the word 'ICED' to mean a small cube used in games.
4. Read the word 'MOOR' backward to mean a space that can be occupied.
5. Read the word 'PACER' backward to mean state again.

SPEED

1. Name the author of the book *Malgudi Days*.
2. What is the most widely spoken language of Brazil?
3. Which royal title are some cobras given?
4. Ajmeri Gate, Kashmiri Gate and Turkman Gate are all located in which Indian city?
5. Which brothers flew the first plane: Wright, Wrong or Maybe?
6. Alexandria is the main port of which country?
7. What is dactyloscopy the science of?
8. What is the larva of a butterfly called?
9. Which one word describes track-and-field events?
10. Which city was formerly called Madinat-al-Salam or City of Peace in Arabic?

ANSWERS

TAKE YOUR PICK

1. Common octopus
2. FIFA World Cup 2002
3. Momo
4. Chola
5. Jharkhand
6. Tabla. Siyahi are the black spots on the tabla.
7. Tamil
8. Milk
9. Amnesty International
10. Ganga

WHAT'S THE QUESTION

1. What is a gerenuk?
2. What are planetoids?
3. Who is Omar Abdullah?
4. What is tapioca?
5. Who was Samuel Morse?
6. Who was King Shantanu?
7. What is a vada?
8. Who was Akela?
9. What is Rath Yatra?
10. What is a dragon?

MIXED BAG

1. Kidney
2. Devika Rani
3. Morarji Desai
4. The Philippines
5. Ostrich
6. Gol Gumbaz
7. Sherlock Holmes
8. Mridangam
9. Manhattan Project
10. Franz Beckenbauer

SPOT THE ANSWER

1. ₹10
2. Taxila
3. Shiva
4. Gestapo
5. Andhra Pradesh

CONFIDENCE ROUND

1. Shekhar Kapur
2. Pigeons
3. Six
4. Joking; it is a ball and socket joint
5. Meghalaya
6. Chaitra
7. Noah
8. Unidentified Flying Object

9. Scrooge
10. Sleet

WHAT'S THE WORD

Set 1
1. Jamshedpur
2. Arm
3. Caped Crusader
4. Karaoke
5. *A Christmas Carol*
6. Latvia
7. JACKAL

Set 2
1. P.V. Narasimha Rao
2. Aamir Khan
3. Christopher Columbus
4. Kulfi
5. Estuary
6. Tweety Pie
7. PACKET

Set 3
1. Twenty years
2. Okra
3. Frigg
4. Form
5. Ear
6. End
7. TOFFEE

Set 4

1. Juhi Chawla
2. International Master
3. Nose
4. Garlic
5. Leonardo da Vinci
6. English
7. JINGLE

Set 5

1. Dragon
2. Origami
3. United Nations
4. Babur
5. Lanka
6. Epicentre
7. DOUBLE

MATHS AND IQ

1. 42

2.
4	Divide	2	Plus	9	Minus	6	=	5

3. Mita

4.
14	Divide	2	Plus	9	Multiply	2	=	32

5. 360 (x2, x3, x4 etc)

VOCABULARY

1. APE
2. SERPENT

3. DICE
4. ROOM
5. RECAP

SPEED

1. R.K. Narayan
2. Portuguese
3. King
4. Delhi
5. Wright
6. Egypt
7. Fingerprint identification
8. A caterpillar
9. Athletics
10. Baghdad